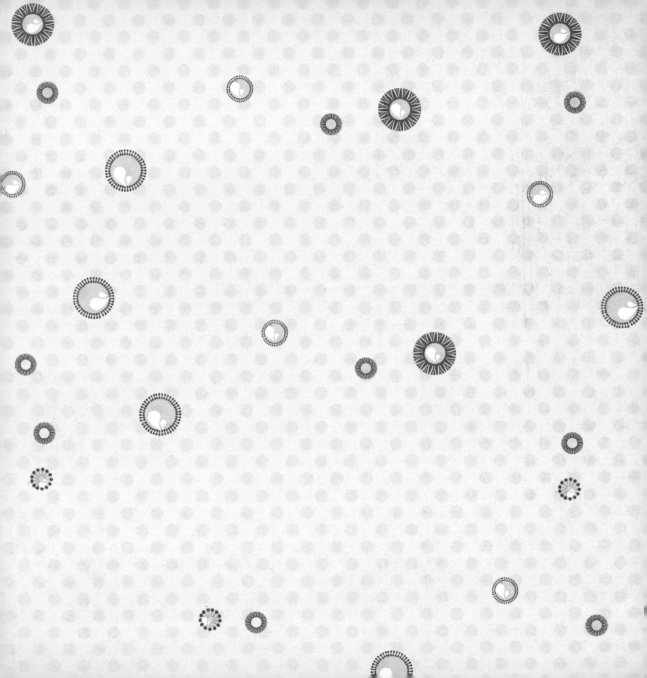

To Brian, the worst liar I know. — cj

Little ✹ BOOST

is published by
Picture Window Books, a Capstone Imprint
1710 Roe Crest Drive
North Mankato, Minnesota 56003
www.capstonepub.com

Library of Congress Cataloging-in-Publication data
is available on the Library of Congress website.

ISBN 978-1-4048-7498-5

Graphic Design: Kay Fraser

Printed in China.
102011
006443

Hello Goodbye

and a very little lie

by Christianne Jones

illustrated by Christine Battuz

PICTURE WINDOW BOOKS
a capstone imprint

Larry is a liar.

"Larry, where are you?" his mom called.

"I'm doing my homework," Larry lied.

"Larry, don't eat all the frosting," his mom said.

"I'm not," Larry lied.

"Larry, why do you lie so much?"

his mom asked.

"I'm not lying,"

Larry replied.

"I'm telling
a tall tale."

"I'm stretching
the truth."

"Oh, Larry," his mom said with a sigh.

"No one is going to listen to you
if you keep lying," his dad said.

"Dad, people always listen to me," Larry said.

At the park, Larry talked
while the others played.

Hello. I'm Larry.
I built this
playground.
GOODBYE.

At the grocery store, Larry stopped
stranger after stranger.

At the library, Larry loudly exclaimed,

Hello. I'm Larry.
I have read
every one of
these books.
GOODBYE.

One sunny Saturday, Larry was on his way
to the beach when he saw a spunky little
girl reading a magazine.

But before he could speed away, the girl
stopped him.

"No, you can't," she said.

"Yes, I CAN,"

Larry said.

"NO, you can't," she said.

"YES, I CAN!" Larry yelled.

"Prove it," she said. "My ball floated to the other side of the lake. Go get it for me."

Larry looked across to the other side
of the lake.

The lake was
REALLY, REALLY BIG.

Larry knew he couldn't swim all the way across the lake.

There was only one thing that Larry could do.

Larry jumped into the water, turned to the small crowd, and declared,

"**GOODBYE,**" said the crowd. And they walked away.

Larry felt all alone, but not for long. The spunky little girl joined him in the water.

"Wait!" Larry yelled.

"Do you think two liars could stop lying and become friends?" Larry asked.

"**No,**" said the girl.

And then she started to laugh.
"That was a lie. Let's
be friends."

And from that day on, Larry never, ever,
EVER told another lie again.